STARRY NIGHT

S T A R R Y
N I G H T

DAVID SPOHN

LOTHROP, LEE & SHEPARD BOOKS
NEW YORK

E
J

for Mom and Dad

Library of Congress Cataloging in Publication Data
Spohn, David. Starry night / by David Spohn.
p.   cm.   Summary: Nate and Matt have a peaceful evening camping out with
their father in the woods behind their house.   ISBN 0-688-11170-X. — ISBN 0-688-11171-8
(lib. bdg.)   [1. Camping—Fiction.]   I. Title.   PZ7.S7635St   1992   [E]—dc20
91-33802   CIP   AC

Nate, Matt, and Dad were going camping.
Not far away.
Just out back at the edge of the pines.
Just out of sight from the house.

Dad got the sleeping bags from the closet.
August had been hot and dry.
The ground would be hard,
so he slipped a pillow into each of them.

Nate gathered the food.
He filled his backpack with cookies
and trail mix, apples and a candy bar
for each of them.

Matt filled the canteens with water.
Then he took Rocky from his bed.
He wrapped him in a small blanket
and tucked him into his backpack.

Dad put his harmonica into his pocket
and handed each boy a flashlight.
It was time to go.
Mom's chickens clucked and scattered
as Dad and the boys stepped off the back porch
and started across the yard.

They hiked past the garden
and out through the tall grass.
Dad led the way,
carefully avoiding sandburs and thistles.
The grass parted where they stepped,
and the cool smell of evening
rose up from the ground.

Where the woods met the open field
was a small clearing.
In its middle was a ring of stones.
Around the stones were stumps to sit on.

They dropped their gear and looked around.
The fire pit was clean and ready,
but there was no wood.
Matt began to gather kindling.
Nate and Dad walked into the pines
to break up fallen limbs.
They brought back enough firewood
to last the night.

Then Matt built the fire;
he knew just what to do.
He built a teepee of small sticks
over a pile of dry grass and pine needles,
then added larger sticks around and around.

Dad lit the fire.
First there was only smoke,
then small flames took hold.
Nate and Matt added more wood
till the fire roared to life.
Then they all stood back and admired their work.
"Let's make ourselves at home," said Dad.
They set their backpacks near the fire
so night critters wouldn't steal their food
and unrolled their sleeping bags.

Dad pulled out his harmonica
and wailed out "Moonshadow."
Next came "Shenandoah."
Then Nate launched into his favorite ghost story:
"Witches' Wood."
Matt held Rocky tight and ate a cookie.
Owls called to one another through the trees.
"Who cooks for you? Who cooks for you?"
they seemed to ask.
A chill ran up Matt's spine.

"Too scary for me!" said Dad.
"Me too," said Matt.
Nate was finished then anyway,
so they all got up to stretch.
As they moved away from the fire,
the sky appeared to grow.
A million shining stars surrounded them.
"Like forever fireflies," said Matt.

Above them was the Big Dipper.
"The Big Dipper is part of
the constellation Ursa Major," said Dad.
"The Great Bear.
He circles the northern sky,
rising in the spring,
swinging low in the fall."
"Is he hunting?" asked Matt.
"Perhaps," said Dad.
"But soon he will rest.
Cassiopeia, the Queen,
will rise to rule the autumn sky."
"Poor bear," said Matt.
"He's probably tired."
He reached up to touch the Great Bear,
and nearly did.

Nate just stood and stared
and dreamed of flying from star to star,
crossing the sky with Ursa Major.
Suddenly a shooting star fell
right where he was looking—
but before he could call out to the others,
it vanished without a trace.
He smiled, knowing it was just for him.

Filled with the magic of the night,
the campers returned to the fire.
They warmed their fronts,
then their back sides.
Together they piled on the last of the wood.
Dad shuffled the coals with a stick
to make the fire last.

Then Nate, Matt, and Dad
climbed into their sleeping bags,
nestling together near the fire.
As the flames burned down,
they settled into a dreamy sleep,
while the Great Bear, Cassiopeia,
and the whole starry night
looked on.